A Case Of
Haida History

Bruce Bradburn
Illustrations by Rhys Haug

Book Publishers Network
P.O. Box 2256
Bothell • WA • 98041
PH • 425-483-3040
www.bookpublishersnetwork.com

Copyright © 2015 by Bruce Bradburn

All rights reserved. No part of this book may be reproduced, stored in, or introduced into a retrieval system, or transmitted in any form, or by any means (electronic, mechanical, photocopying, recording, or otherwise) without the prior written permission of the publisher.

10 9 8 7 6 5 4 3 2 1

Printed in the United States of America

LCCN 2015932183
ISBN 978-1-940598-63-5

Editor: Julie Scandora
Cover design: Laura Zugzda
Interior design: Melissa Vail Coffman
Production: Scott Book

Hole-in-the-Wall
Octopus Islands
Marine Park
Maurelle
Island
Okisollo Channel
Whiterock Pass
Surge
Narrows
Quadra
Island
Village
Bay
Lake
Hoskyn Channel
Read
Island
Bold
Island
Chinese
Mountains
Seymour Narrows
Breton
Islands
Hyacinthe Bay
Heriot
Bay
Sutil Channel
Discovery Passage
Rebecca Spit
April
Point
Quathiaski
Cove
Cape
Mudge
Lighthouse

Acknowledgements

The author wishes to acknowledge over forty years of close friendship with Nat and Linda Collier and their contribution in providing the exposure to the regions described in this book. Through voyages over the past twenty-plus years on their boats *Sunbird* and *Reflections* they have explored extensively the territory chronicled in the journey of Will and Michael with Harold and Jane, and the author has been privileged to have accompanied them on several of these sojourns.

The author also wishes to thank Robert Bringhurst for his input in developing the concept of creating a "new" Haida legend.

A special thank-you to the entire crew at Book Publishers Network for their advice and assistance, without which this book could not have been brought to print.

Prologue

Several lifetimes ago, in the manner men measure time, Great Spirit called unto himself Eagle.

"I have become concerned that the lesson I taught my people with K'iid K'iyass may not serve their future generations. Many new people have come into the land of Haida Gwaii and are taking more from the land and sea than they need. I fear for our forests, our waters, our salmon and other fish, and all our birds and beasts. I even fear for K'iid K'iyass himself."

"But, Great Spirit," responded Eagle, "can't you simply force these new people to obey your commands?"

"They do not listen. I also fear that these newcomers will corrupt my people as well."

"If you do not have the power to control these things," asked Eagle, "what can I possibly do?"

"I need you to take on a special quest," responded Great Spirit. "Fly to K'iid K'iyass. At the very top of the Golden Spruce, you will find an unusual cone. Take this cone in your talons and fly southward from Haida Gwaii until you find an archipelago of many islands in the rain shadow of a very large island. I will guide you to one of these islands upon which there is no human habitation. At a point high on this island, in a clearing, you will break open the cone and spread the seeds you find therein around the clearing."

"I will do exactly as you have instructed," said Eagle. "When I have done this, will our forests and waters and wild creatures be safe?"

"Only time can answer that, my friend," said Great Spirit. "We can hope, but men are so foolish, and their power for self-destruction seems limitless."

"If it were only their self-destruction that was the result of their foolishness, the rest of us might well survive," observed Eagle.

"An astute conclusion," replied Great Spirit. "But the actions of men are never simply confined to their own species. Now it is time for you to embark on this important mission. I shall watch over you and speed your flight."

"Thank you, Great Spirit. I go with resolve and in hope."

Chapter One

It was raining in Seattle, an event that did not make the first section of any newspaper in any country of the world. Michael looked out his bedroom window at the rivulets streaming down the pane and mused about summer and his family's annual journey to their home on Quadra Island in British Columbia, Canada.

Even with another full quarter of school left before the long summer break, Michael and his cousin, Will, in Chicago, had been in constant email communication making plans for how to spend their time together on the island. Last year they had both passed the tests and received their boating licenses, and their parents had let them take a couple of trips on their own. They were already laying out where they would take the Whaler on cruises and overnight camping.

In each of the last two summers, the boys had crossed paths with several groups of rather rough characters, and this summer they were hoping just to be able to enjoy more relaxing adventures. Both sets of parents were hoping the same thing.

Michael's mother, Angie, rapped gently on his door and came into his room.

"Watching the rain doesn't seem to be getting any numbers on that page of math problems," she observed, glancing at the blank worksheet on his desk.

"I know," Michael responded. "But I was just thinking about the summer. Will and I have been going over plans for some trips we want to take. Do you think we can take off in the boat on our own again?"

"Well, you both handled yourselves quite well last year. I don't think that will be a problem. However, please realize that the adults may want to have some time with it as well."

"No problem there. Besides we have the kayaks for shorter trips, and we may just want to bike to some campsites right on Quadra."

"I'm pleased you and Will are getting your plans in order, but you still have schoolwork to do before you are free for the summer."

"Oh, I know. I also have crew workouts. We should have a really good team this year, and I want to do well there, too."

"I'm sure you won't let either of those tasks slide. We'll try to head north very soon after you get out of school. Your father has already put his work schedule in order so we can have a nice vacation. Doug and Judy will come out for at least a couple of weeks, but they've told us that Will is all set for spending the entire summer, so you should have plenty of time to get in all the activities you have planned."

"OK, I'll get back on the math right now. By the way, what's for dinner?"

"Short ribs, mashed potatoes, and green beans. I also made a fresh batch of brownies. You must really have been off in space; you didn't come bounding into the kitchen the moment they came out of the oven."

"I guess I was a little lost in thought, but I'll make up for it later."

"I'm sure you will!"

Chapter Two

Will sat looking out his bedroom window at the expanse of Lake Michigan stretching off to the horizon forty stories below. He enjoyed the water vista but missed the sight of trees, islands, and mountains that he had at his cousin's place in British Columbia. He fell into a reverie thinking of the special times he had had there over the last two years and the perilous adventures he and Michael had shared. He was completely lost in his thoughts and dreams of future adventures when his father came into the room.

"Having a good daydream?" his father asked.

"Huh? Oh, I guess so. Just thinking of Quadra."

"I know what you mean. It's hard to get it out of my thoughts, too."

"Do you think we'll be heading out west again the summer?"

"Bob and Angie have already asked that we come out and have invited you for the entire summer. You and Michael really have hit it off, haven't you?"

"Absolutely, but I do remember my initial reaction about spending even a month with him a couple of years ago. I would guess he probably felt the same way at the time, but we've put that VERY far behind us."

"I assume, then, that you are all for the summer plan."

"Just try and stop me from going!"

"I wouldn't dream of it, but we have a few months to make plans, and I assume you and Michael will have a pretty full agenda before we get there. You both handled the boat extremely well last summer, so I imagine you'll want to have a few new trips."

"We've emailed about that. I know we want to take the boat into Squirrel Cove over on Cortes Island. We walked over from Von Donop Inlet on our first overnight last year, but we couldn't actually get to the main part of the cove since the trail came out in really gooey mud flats we couldn't walk across."

"Uncle Bob has told us about the cove, and your mom and I would also like to see it. Maybe what we could do is all go over in the Whaler and tow the two-person kayak loaded with your tent and food for a couple of days. You two could camp out and have the kayak to get around, and then we would come back over and pick you up."

"That might work out just fine. I'll bounce the idea off Michael. We'll also need a few bucks because Michael says there's an old guy who makes fantastic cinnamon buns on a float house in the cove, and we wouldn't want to miss those."

"Knowing you two, I can't imagine your missing a meal of any kind," said his dad with a smile. "When you hear back from Michael, let me know, and I'll contact Uncle Bob."

"Will do."

"By the way, how's school going? Your last report was quite good."

"Well, the studies aren't getting any easier, but they're pretty interesting, especially social studies."

"Really? That wouldn't have anything to do with your study mate, would it?"

"C'mon, Dad, we're just friends, but she is pretty cute, and smart, too. Our teacher is finishing up the year again with a unit on the Native Americans of both the US and Canada, and we've both really enjoyed doing research. We're doing a joint paper on the Haida."

"That's very interesting. I'd love to read it when you're finished. You also have baseball ramping up, right?"

"Yup. I tried out for third base on the varsity team, and the coach was happy with my workout, so I'm hoping to nail down that spot."

"Good luck on that. Keep me posted. Do you have any major homework assignments over this weekend?"

Chapter Two

"Just some reading and a bit of math. Mostly it will be research on the paper. I'm going to email Michael to see if he or Uncle Bob has any good ideas for it."

"Well, I'll let you get to that. We'll call you for dinner."

Chapter Three

Michael was just finishing up his math when his computer let him know that an email had arrived. He penciled in the last answer on the worksheet and checked his inbox.

Hi cuz,

How's everything? I was just talking with my dad about going up to Quadra again this summer. I'm already hyped. Anyway, he thought maybe we could have our parents drop us and all our camping gear and food off in Squirrel Cove, so they could have a chance to see it, and then pick us up a few days later. How does that sit with you, assuming they give us enough money for those cinnamon rolls?

I also have another question for either you or your dad about the Haida. Remember those great argillite carvings we saw at the BC Museum last summer in Victoria? My social studies teacher is doing another unit on Native Americans for this last quarter, and I want to do a paper on the Haida. Do you know of any sources for inside information on the tribe? By the

Chapter Three

way, that cute girl in my class is working with me on this project.

Let me know what you find out. Thanks much.

Will

Thinking this would make a good subject for conversation over dinner, Michael went back to watching the rain run down his window and thought about doing the reading he had been assigned.

When his forehead bounced off his computer keyboard, he looked down at his watch and realized that it was almost dinnertime. Rubbing his eyes and stretching, he rose from his chair and headed toward the kitchen. He could hear his parents talking over the day's events, and the delicious smells of his mother's cooking worked their way into his nose and brain.

"Hi, guys," he said cheerfully as he entered the room.

"Hi, yourself," replied his father. "What have you been up to today?"

"I did my math and got an email from Will, but mostly, I just watched the rain—at least until I fell asleep."

"What's up with Will?" asked his mother.

"He wanted to know if it might be all right for the two of us to do a camping trip at Squirrel Cove this summer. He said his dad suggested that the four of you could take us over in the Whaler and tow the two-man kayak along. You could drop us off with our gear and then come back in a couple days and pick us up."

"I think that could work," said his father.

"Judy and I had talked last year about getting her and Doug over to see the cove, and that would be a good way to work it in for all of us," put in Angie.

"You can certainly tell Will that's fine with us," said his father. "I'll confirm it with Uncle Doug."

"That's great!" said Michael. "There would be some money available for cinnamon buns, wouldn't there?"

"Don't worry," said Angie, "we won't let you starve."

"Will also had another question, and I don't have a ready answer for him, but maybe the two of you do. He's doing a paper on the Haida for his social studies class and wanted to know if we could suggest any good research materials."

"Wow! This is totally weird," said Bob. "I was just talking at work this week with a man who is planning a trip up north this summer and had been doing some research himself into the First Nations people. He knew we had a place on Quadra Island and asked if I knew one of our neighbors, a Robert Bringhurst. I told him I didn't know anything about Mr. Bringhurst, and he gave me a brief rundown on the man. I Googled Robert Bringhurst later and found out he lives just down the road from us and is probably the most influential living Canadian poet. He's published over a dozen books of poetry, about as many in prose, and has done a number of significant translations. He's written several books specifically on the Haida. Let's go over to the computer and take a look."

Dinner was put on hold as the family gathered around the screen learning about their famous neighbor. Michael was fascinated. He pointed out to his parents that one of the books Mr. Bringhurst had written was with a man named Bill Reid who was a renowned native carver and that he and Will had seen several of his carvings at the museum in Victoria. There was far more material than they could assimilate, but Michael said he would email Will right after dinner and tell him where to go to get started on the research for his paper.

What with the intellectual stimulation and the delay in serving, Michael found himself ravenously hungry. Two full helpings of everything and probably the largest single brownie ever carved out of a pan, smothered in giant scoops of vanilla ice cream, finally filled him up.

"Do you think that will hold you until bedtime?" asked his mother.

"I think so," he responded. "But you might want to put what's left of the brownies out of sight so there are some left for tomorrow."

With that, he went off to his room to compose his email to Will. Michael knew that with the two-hour time difference his cousin would probably not read his email until tomorrow, so he took his time and tried to include everything he had learned about the man on

Chapter Three

Quadra who could be a wealth of information on the subject for Will's paper. After nearly an hour of typing, he finally summed up:

> Well, cuz, that's about all I know at this point, but you can do a more extensive Google search on Robert Bringhurst and get in touch with him directly.
>
> Two of his books sound really interesting, and I think I'll try to pick them up for myself. The one he did with Bill Reid is *The Raven Steals the Light,* and another one of his translations is *Masterworks of the Classical Haida Mythtellers*. Both sound as if they could be good sources for your paper, and I'd bet you'd impress both your "study mate" and your teacher.
>
> Good luck,
> Michael

Having put himself in a mindset of reading, Michael flopped on his bed with his reading homework assignment.

Chapter Four

Will was taking advantage of Sunday morning by sleeping in, having remembered to turn off his alarm. He had made up his mind when he turned out his light the night before that he would forego breakfast and home in on a big brunch. He didn't have anything to do until two o'clock when he planned to meet some friends in the park for baseball practice and a game of 500.

After an extended and very deep sleep, he rolled out of bed, grabbed his robe, and headed for the kitchen to see if he could talk his mother into feeding him. Otherwise, it would just be multiple bowls of cereal, which was not really his idea of a big brunch. Luckily he found his mother at her computer in the kitchen.

"Good morning, Mom, at least I think it's still morning."

"You just made it. It's eleven fifty-five."

"Is there an off chance you might whip up a little brunch for your favorite son?"

"I suppose that can be arranged. Just let me finish this email. What did you have in mind?"

"Oh, I don't know. Maybe some waffles, sausage patties, and a couple of fried eggs."

"Is that all? How about some homemade corned beef hash and fresh blueberry muffins on the side?"

"That would be great! Did you make the muffins this morning?"

Chapter Four

"I'm just kidding about the hash and muffins. Try to make do with the rest of your order."

"All right. Besides I don't want to be too weighed down. I've got an informal baseball practice with some friends at two."

"OK. Go get dressed, and I'll start on your little snack."

"Thanks, Mom."

Will went back to his room, dressed, and put out the gear he needed to take to practice. He fired up his computer to see if he had a message from his cousin and was amazed at the length. He was still avidly reading Michael's email when his mother came to his door.

"You don't want the waffles to get cold, do you?"

"Oh, gosh, Mom, I completely lost track of time. I emailed Michael about some possible sources for material for my paper on the Haida, and he sent me practically a whole book."

"Why don't you come to the kitchen? You can tell me about it while you eat."

"I'm on my way."

Will settled down in front of a stack of waffles topped by two fried eggs, with a couple of sausage patties hanging over the side of the plate. Between mouthfuls, he told his mother about Michael's email.

"Before I leave for practice, I'm going to look up Robert Bringhurst and see if there's contact information for him. It's amazing that he lives right up the road from Michael on Quadra and has all this firsthand info on the Haida."

"That is fascinating. I hope you can get to meet him during your stay this summer."

"Me, too. I have about a half-hour before I need to catch the bus to the park, so I guess I'll go to my room and do some work. Thanks for the brunch, Mom. I'm pretty sure I can make it through till dinner."

"THAT remains to be seen. I might just have a small snack when you get back from baseball."

"You're the best!"

The next thirty minutes seemed to fly by for Will. There was so much information he didn't know where to start. He did find an email address for Robert Bringhurst and decided to send him a brief message asking for any direction regarding what to take up in his paper. He sent it off and just had time to grab his gear and head out the door for the bus.

"See you in a few hours," he yelled over his shoulder as he ran out the door and headed for the elevator.

Chapter Five

Will arrived home about five, and true to her word, his mother had laid out an apple and some cheese and crackers on the kitchen table to tide him over till dinner. Neither of his parents was around, so he took the snack with him to his bedroom, stowed his baseball gear in the footlocker, and fired up his computer.

He was quite surprised to see that he had received an email from Robert Bringhurst.

> Dear Will,
>
> Thank you very much for the email regarding your desire to write a paper on the Haida for your social studies class. They are a fascinating people and culture. I don't know exactly how long you plan on making your paper, but I think it would be best to concentrate on one aspect of their culture, unless you plan on spending several years writing.
>
> For a high school paper, you might find researching one or more of the many myths and legends the Haida have as their history. As you may have already discovered, theirs is an oral society with no formal written language. You mentioned in your email my

book written with Bill Reid, who, unfortunately, is no longer with us, *The Raven Steals the Light*. The book is a translation of ten such myths, most relating to the Raven, who is one of the most important creatures in their culture, as well as in many other tribes.

Telling several of these stories and then explaining how each relates to the Haida culture could be an interesting paper for your teacher and classmates.

With the amazing power of the Internet, your research will be far easier than it would have been even a few years ago, but do take the time to verify your facts from more than one source. The Haida Nation does have its own website, which tells you a little about where we are going, and I would recommend you start there to pick out what myths or legends you wish to put into your paper.

I am gratified that there is an interest in the First Nations people in high schools in the United States, especially as far away as the Midwest. If I can be of further assistance as you proceed, please do not hesitate to contact me.

Very truly yours,

Robert Bringhurst

    Will was blown away that a renowned author would take the time to respond in such length and detail. He could hardly wait to tell Michael and his parents, but first he had a phone call to make. She answered on the second ring.
    "I couldn't wait till tomorrow to tell you some really cool news," Will blurted out after a hurried "hello."
    "I assume it has something to do with our paper."

Chapter Five

"Absolutely. I emailed my cousin in Seattle about getting some inside information on the Haida, and it turns out that one of the world's greatest experts on them lives just down the road from my cousin's place on Quadra Island."

"What a weird coincidence," she replied.

"Not only that, but I found an email address for him and sent him a message that we were doing a paper on the Haida, and I just got this amazing reply from him!"

"That's great. What did he say?"

"He suggested we pick out a couple of the Haida myths or legends and explain how they influence their society. He's written a book on some of them, and I'm going to get a copy ASAP. He also told me about a website that the Haida Nation has set up and said that would be a good place to start our research."

"Maybe we can get together after school tomorrow and check it out. How's your schedule?"

"I don't have baseball practice tomorrow, so why don't we just meet in the computer lab after our last class so we can have multiple searches going on?"

"That's a super plan! See you tomorrow."

Will rang off, finished his snack, and was just taking his dishes to the kitchen when his parents came in the door.

"Wow," he said, "this social studies paper is going to be the best ever! I got a reply from Robert Bringhurst with some really great ideas, and my study mate and I are getting together tomorrow after school to start the research. When's dinner?"

Chapter Six

The school year for Michael was rapidly coming to an end. His crew team had an exceptional year and went to several regattas in the area, gathering a number of trophies. As usual, he also excelled at his studies and had even found time to pick up the books he had tracked down for his cousin and actually read them. He and Will had emailed several times about the books and exchanged ideas.

In their emails, Will had mentioned that his research had shown a lot of information was kept at the Anthropological Museum on the University of British Columbia campus in Vancouver. The boys decided to ask their parents if this summer they could all get together in Vancouver before Will and his parents went up to Quadra.

The idea was greeted with enthusiasm by both sets of parents. Doug checked with his club in Chicago and found out it had a reciprocal relationship with the Vancouver Club, so he made arrangements for both families to stay there for a few days. The Chicago group made reservations to fly directly into Vancouver. Bob, Angie, and Michael would drive down from Quadra, and they would all drive back together to the island.

Meanwhile, in Chicago, Will and his study mate were hard at work researching their paper on the Haida. They had selected several myths regarding Raven and had assembled an impressive array of stories showing how intricately this creature was woven into the culture. They both found the research and writing of the paper to be invigorating and spent many hours polishing the wording and choosing just the right illustrations. The paper earned both of them solid As on the paper itself and in the class as a whole

Will did get the third base spot on the varsity baseball team and had a very good year. The team won their league championship and even got through the first round of the state tournament before falling to the eventual winner of the entire tournament.

Chapter Six

Michael's family left for Quadra a few days after school ended and spent over a week getting everything in order for the summer. The Whaler was de-winterized, the kayaks washed and waxed, the furniture and barbeque taken out of storage and put on the deck, and the main house and caboose made spic and span.

The huckleberries were just getting ripe, and Michael was able to get several quarts picked and frozen so they could have a pie when they all came up from Vancouver. The SUV was packed up, and the family headed down to Nanaimo for the ferry ride to Vancouver. This trip they opted for the run from Departure Bay to Horseshoe Bay instead of their normal route going to and from Seattle.

Will's family had an uneventful flight from O'Hare to Vancouver, gathered their limited baggage, cleared Customs, and grabbed a cab to downtown. When they arrived at the Vancouver Club, they found the other group was just checking in. After hugs and handshakes, they all retired to their rooms to freshen up and then meet in the lobby for dinner.

Chapter Seven

The concierge at the Vancouver Club provided them with a short list of good family dining spots within walking distance. The boys picked the restaurant, and they set off for a leisurely stroll.

"I think you'll find Vancouver quite different from Victoria," Bob mentioned as they walked along. "It's far larger and much more cosmopolitan, being the financial center of Western Canada. Even though Victoria is the capital of the province, Vancouver is really the hub of activity. Angie and I haven't spent a lot of time here, but we do have a few 'don't miss' places."

"We definitely want to get to the Anthropological Museum," put in Will.

"Oh, it's an absolute must see," said Bob. "We should take a drive out there tomorrow morning. The UBC campus is huge and really beautiful, and there're some great views of the city from there. If we start early enough, on the way back to town, we can hit Granville Island. If you liked the Pike Place Market in Seattle, then you'll love the market there."

The group arrived at their restaurant and were early enough to get a table for the six of them right away. After placing their orders, Bob brought out a map of the city he had picked up at the club and went over some of the other places they needed to see in their rather limited time.

Chapter Seven

"We should get out to Stanley Park. If you boys haven't seen enough totem poles after the museum, you can see many more in the park."

"Oh, we need to have lunch at the Teahouse," said Angie. "Both the food and the views are great!"

"The aquarium is also fantastic, as are the gardens," said Bob. "If we start at the park first thing in the morning day after tomorrow, we can drive up to North Vancouver in the afternoon and take in the Capilano Bridge."

"I've heard of that bridge," said Doug. "It's supposed to be spectacular."

"There're a couple of things to do there as well as walking the bridge over the river. The Cliffwalk and Treetops Adventure are truly great experiences. If we hit these, I think that will give you at least an overview of the city," said Bob. "Of course, we won't have been able to get to a number of other sights in Vancouver, such as Robson Strasse, Canada Place, Gastown, and Chinatown."

"Hopefully, this will just give you another reason to make future trips here," put in Angie.

"I don't think there is any danger of our not being interested in future trips," said Judy, a sentiment readily agreed to by Doug and Will.

Their dinners arrived, and conversation was put on hold while both families dug in. During the brief respite between dinner and dessert, Bob made another announcement.

"I just received this information this morning, so I haven't even had a chance to share it with Angie and Michael. I got a call from some old friends of ours from Seattle who have a lovely large cruiser. They'll be coming up north in about ten days and stopping by our place on Quadra. They usually have their own grandchildren with them, but theirs happen to have other plans for this summer, and they asked if Michael would like to join them for a trip farther north. I told them Will would also be with us, and they said they would be delighted to have two young crew members for their trip."

"You couldn't even mention this on the drive down?" asked Michael.

"We got to talking about everything we wanted to do in Vancouver, and it just slipped my mind," responded his father.

"Where are they headed?" asked Michael.

"They said they did want to get to Mamalilaculla, and I thought both you boys would like to see the site of the last potlatch, what with your interest in the First Nations cultures."

"Wow! That would be fantastic," said Will.

"We could never get there in the Whaler," put in Michael. "This would be really fun."

"Well, just remember you'll be crew, so you'll need to take orders from the skipper and first mate."

"Do you think we'll have time for the camping trip to Squirrel Cove before they arrive?" asked Michael.

"I don't see why not," responded his father. "We have the two days here and most of the third getting back to Quadra, but you were talking about a two-night trip to the cove, so we should be able to work it all in easily."

"Then you folks can have the Whaler all to yourselves for a week or so, which should make everyone happy," said Michael with a grin.

Chapter Eight

The next two days in Vancouver seemed like a blur. Thanks to Bob's careful planning, the families were able to hit the four attractions he had laid out over dinner.

The trip to the museum was a huge hit. The totems and carvings were both numerous and excellent. The boys found a few of the works of Bill Reid and pointed them out to their parents. They also explored many items that were not on display but in the glass-enclosed storage areas by using the computer terminals to look up items they wanted to see and then getting the exact location in the storage area where they could be viewed.

The drive through the UBC campus was like going through a park, and the views back toward the downtown area were spectacular. They spent almost three hours before heading back to Granville Island. By the time they got there, the boys were making serious "lunch" noises, so the first stop was at one of the many restaurant choices available. Once the hollow legs of two teenage lads were at least partially filled, they proceeded to check out the market, which was just as much fun and varied as the Pike Place Market in Seattle.

Meats, seafood, cheese, vegetables, breads, and a huge variety of other food and non-food items were beautifully displayed. Judy and Angie found a few items of hand-crafted jewelry that simply HAD to be purchased.

By the time they had explored the island and made their way back to the Vancouver Club, it was almost time for dinner. The concierge at the club gave them some more suggestions for dinner, and they picked out one that was again close enough for a short walk. After taking an hour or so to freshen up, they made the walk and enjoyed another wonderful meal with animated conversation about what they were to see the next day.

The next morning, after breakfast at the club, they drove to Stanley Park and made straight to the aquarium and spent over an hour enjoying the exhibits. After a short trip through the gardens and a look at the many totems, they drove down to the Teahouse for lunch. As was advertised by Angie, the food and views were great.

After lunch, they headed over Lion's Gate Bridge and on to Capilano Park for a walk on the bridge. They entered the park and opted for the bridge walk, the Cliffwalk, and the Treetops Adventure. Both families greatly enjoyed the walk across the bridge, in spite of the fact that the boys tried to sway the bridge. Both the Cliffwalk and Treetops were totally spectacular and thrilling for all.

Making their way back to the club, they decided simply to dine there that evening and make it an early night so they could get on the road to Quadra early the next day.

All in all, the Vancouver adventure had been a wonderful experience for everyone, and they were primed for the next stage on Quadra.

Chapter Nine

The families got an early start the next morning over Lion's Gate Bridge and on to Horseshoe Bay for the ferry to Nanaimo. The boys were not pleased with leaving before breakfast, but they were promised a full meal on board during the cruise north.

As they pulled into the terminal, Will said, "Look, Dad, that's the big ferry we saw on our first flight to Quadra two years ago!"

The ferry was painted with sports scenes honoring the province's hosting of the Winter Olympics in 2010. Bob gave them a few facts about the vessel.

"That's the *Coastal Renaissance*, one of the largest ferries in the fleet. She's 520 feet long and can hold 370 cars, including thirty-two semis, and can carry over sixteen-hundred passengers and crew."

"Wow!" exclaimed Will. "She makes the Quadra Island ferry look like a lifeboat and the Cortes ferry like a dinghy."

"I'm sure you and Michael will be glad to hear that this one has a full restaurant, so you can eat all the way to Nanaimo," said Angie with a smile.

The crossing from the mainland to Vancouver Island took about an hour and a half, and the boys did, indeed, eat almost the entire journey. They did leave their table to rush on deck to look at a pod of orcas the crew announced were passing off the port bow. The ferry slowed so everyone could get a good view but kept a respectable distance away.

"...to look at a pod of orcas..."

Chapter Nine

After docking at the terminal in Departure Bay, they wound up the hill through a residential neighborhood, then onto a highway with more commercial buildings, and finally joined the Inland Island Highway north of the downtown area of Nanaimo.

The hour-and-a-half drive to Campbell River was uneventful, and they arrived at the ferry dock just in time to make the ferry to Quadra. A half-hour later, they pulled into the driveway. After unpacking the car, Angie and Judy announced they would put together some sandwiches for lunch and start making plans for dinner.

The boys hurried off to the caboose, which was their private bunkhouse, to get settled in but assured their parents they would return shortly. After the sandwiches had been completely consumed, along with an entire bag of chips, a couple of cans of soda, and about a dozen cookies, they decided to take the kayaks out for a paddle around Hyacinthe Bay.

The sun was warm on their backs as they ventured out to the seal rocks, and by the time they had explored Open Bay and returned to the float, they were pretty sweaty. Feeling the water, they decided it was warm enough to warrant a quick dip. They stowed the kayaks, ran to the caboose to change, returned to the float, and jumped off the end without a second thought.

The second thought came immediately after they hit the water. Once below the top few inches, the water temperature dropped at least fifteen degrees. However, since neither of them wanted to be the first to give up on the swim, they both stayed in the water until their bodies had adjusted to the chill and their teeth had stopped chattering. After splashing around for a while, the idea of just stretching out on the deck seemed very appealing, so they climbed out, dried off, and made their way to the main house.

Chapter Ten

That night at dinner, the conversation turned to the trip to Squirrel Cove on Cortes Island. All decided to spend the next day getting everything ready so they could depart the following day. Angie and Judy assured the boys there would be plenty of nourishment in the cooler, and Bob and Doug came up with money for the cinnamon buns. The boys said they would assemble a few clothes to take and get the tent and their sleeping bags packed into the two-man kayak, which they would tow over to the cove.

With the plans firmly in mind, it was determined that a farewell Monopoly game was in order. While Angie, Judy, and the boys cleared the table and did the dishes, Bob and Doug set up the board and doled out the money.

The game lasted longer than usual, but in typical fashion, Doug finally emerged victorious to the combined groans of the other five. Since it had been a rather long travel day, they all decided one game was enough, and everyone headed for bed, ready to make preparations in the morning for the adventure to Squirrel Cove.

After a hearty breakfast, the boys set about putting their gear in order. They took the tent, sleeping bags, and a small cook stove down to the boathouse to make sure they would fit into the hatches on the kayak. There was still plenty of room for the few items of clothing they were bringing, the paddles, and their personal flotation devices, or PFDs. The jam-packed cooler would ride with them in the Whaler.

Chapter Ten

Angie and Judy put together two easily-heated dinners and plenty of fixings for lunches and snacks but included just the bare necessities for breakfasts knowing the boys would probably overdose on cinnamon buns at the little bakery in the cove.

Bob and Doug took the boat down to the marina in Heriot Bay and filled the gas tank and two spare cans. The adults planned to do a little exploring on their own after dropping the boys and their gear off in Squirrel Cove.

With preparations made and everything ready to simply load onto the Whaler in the morning, everyone took it easy for the rest of the afternoon. Michael and Will found a patch of big, ripe huckleberries, and with a promise from Angie that she would make a pie for dessert, they spent a couple of hours picking several quarts of berries, about half of which they froze for future treats.

Dinner that night was a big barbeque with special homemade sausages from the market in Heriot Bay, potato salad, corn on the cob, and of course, the huckleberry pie smothered in ice cream. After dinner, Doug threw out a challenge for another Monopoly game. With some misgivings, the rest of the crew agreed, and the game began in earnest.

For a change, Doug could not get any good rolls, and he had to struggle not to be the first one out. Finally, Michael eliminated all remaining players in one circuit of the board and headed to bed with a feeling of accomplishment. He crowed all the way down to the caboose until Will threatened him with serious bodily harm.

Chapter Eleven

The next morning, they could not have had a more perfect day for a boat trip. A check of the weather forecast showed the same for the next five days. After a quick breakfast, they all made their way down to the float and loaded the Whaler for the journey.

It was a little crowded for the six of them, but the boys sat on the cooler, and the kayak was tied on behind, so everyone was reasonably comfortable. They decided to go around the north end of Cortes on their way to Squirrel Cove so Doug and Judy could see Von Donop Inlet, where the boys made their first overnight trip in the boat last summer.

It was a bit of a run around the north end of Cortes and down the Lewis Channel to the entrance of Squirrel Cove, and they were all happy to come around Protection Island and into the cove. It was still early enough in the season that the cove was not totally jammed with boats, so they easily cruised around and explored.

They discovered a very small islet near the end of the cove, and the boys thought that would be a perfect place for their camp. No one else had settled in on it, so they had the place to themselves. They beached the Whaler and pulled the kayak up onto the shore. The boys quickly unpacked the tent and set it up, staking their claim. They found a cool place to stash the cooler and put the little cook stove by the tent.

Chapter Eleven

Bob pointed to the end of the cove near the islet and informed the boys that there was a very shallow channel that connected the cove to a salt-water lagoon, which had another little islet in it.

"I think you two will find it fun to ride the rapids in the channel at tide changes," said Bob. "You can do it in your PFDs, but it might be a tad tricky in the kayak."

With that, they reboarded the Whaler and toured the rest of the cove. Just opposite the entrance, there was a float with a ramp up to a small store, which also had a deli in it. They grabbed some sandwiches and drinks and had a leisurely lunch watching the other boaters.

When they finished eating, Bob announced that they would take the boys back to the campsite and the adults would take off for a circumnavigation of Cortes. On the way back to the islet, Bob pointed out the building on a log raft that housed the bakery. He told the boys they should paddle over right away and place their order for tomorrow morning.

"It's now about two," Bob informed them all. "We have just enough time to get around the south end of the island and up to Gorge Harbor. As a surprise, I booked us a couple of rooms at a lodge at the marina, so we can have our own overnight."

"We also made reservations at the restaurant in the marina, so we can have a lovely meal and a peaceful evening," added Angie.

"And we don't have to have another Monopoly game, either," said Judy, laughing.

Michael and Will were dropped off at their islet camp, and their parents motored out of the cove, into Desolation Sound, and down the coast of Cortes, headed south.

The boys took a few minutes to unpack the rest of their gear from the kayak and make their camp ready for evening and then donned their PFDs, climbed aboard, and headed to the bakery.

They found the baker, who looked to be as crusty as his products, sitting on his porch puffing on his pipe. In spite of his gruff appearance, he greeted the boys warmly.

"We'd like to order four cinnamon buns for both tomorrow morning and the morning after," said Michael. "When can we pick them up?"

"Any time after about 7:30," he replied. "Would you like to take a look around where I do the baking?"

"Sure!" replied Will, eagerly.

"Come on in."

The boys followed him into the house on the float and saw that almost the entire ground floor was a kitchen with a huge granite table for rolling out dough and four ovens. A large mixer sat on one end of a counter, and bins below it were filled with flour. Above the counter were shelves containing the biggest jars of cinnamon and sugar the boys had ever seen.

"Wow, you must make a lot of cinnamon buns," exclaimed Michael.

"During the peak of the summer, I turn out over forty dozen a day," he replied. "I get up around four in the morning to start the batches of dough, heat up the ovens, and mix the cinnamon and sugar for the filling. I go through a little bit of butter, as well," he said opening a refrigerator, jammed with tubs of butter.

"You must love what you do," observed Will.

"Well, I do enjoy it, but the best part is all the interesting people I get to meet. I've some boaters who've been coming here for about twenty years, but there's a bunch of new ones every year."

"Do you do this all the time?" asked Michael.

"No, just in the summer. I head south in the winter for a little R&R and a break from the ovens."

"We'll pay you now for both days," said Michael. "And we'll be here bright and early tomorrow morning."

"I'll look forward to seeing you. By the way, I had a couple of buns left from this morning's batches. Take them along with you, on me, for a little snack."

"Gee, thanks!" both boys said gleefully.

They bid the baker farewell and headed back to their camp to stow the buns away for their evening dessert. They paddled past the camp to check out the channel into the lagoon and noticed the water was very low and not moving, so they decided to rest up and wait for the tide to change.

Chapter Twelve

As the tide came in over the shallow rocky bottom, the water warmed enough that the boys donned their PFDs and swam over to the channel into the lagoon. Their first run through the rapids was exciting. The rocks on the bottom had been worn so smooth by the tidal flows that even when they bumped into one they simply slid over it without getting scratched.

Once in the lagoon, they could see the little island in the middle but decided it was a bit far for a swim, so they decided to watch to see if there was a time when there would be enough water in the channel to allow them to bring the kayak through.

They had to hike back up the channel to the cove in order to make another run, and by now there were other people doing the same thing. They made three more runs during the next hour and then just lay in the sun to dry off and check out the water level. In another hour, it appeared there was plenty of water to allow the kayak to pass through, but by now it was approaching dinner time, so they swam back to camp, set up the cook stove, and picked out what they wanted for their evening meal.

The choice of mac and cheese or spaghetti and meatballs was a tough one, so they just flipped a coin, and the macaroni won. They fired up the stove, wrapped it in foil for a little oven, and started heating the dish. They also warmed up some carrots their mothers had packed, and planned on the cinnamon buns to finish off.

"The next incoming tide like this will be in about twelve hours," observed Michael, "so we can go get our fresh buns tomorrow morning and have some breakfast before running the rapids in the kayak."

"We'll have to spend a couple of hours in the lagoon," said Will. "I'd much rather ride the outgoing tide through the channel than have to carry the kayak back."

"I'm with you on that," said Michael enthusiastically. "Besides, I want to paddle out to the island in the lagoon anyway."

"We should have plenty of time for that and a little exploring," said Will. "But I think dinner must be ready. Let's dig in!"

After finishing off the entire casserole of mac and cheese, the carrots, and the cinnamon buns, and a quart of milk, they cleaned up their dishes and packed them away. Then both boys lay back on their sleeping bags and surveyed the scene before them. There were now about half a dozen boats at their end of the cove, but everyone had anchored leaving a lot of room for privacy. Since they were on the east side of Cortes, the sun had gone down over the top of the island. Although still quite light, the temperature had started to cool down.

They moved their sleeping bags into the tent to watch the moon rise but were sound asleep before it made it much above the horizon.

The next morning, the sun had the boys up and about early, and they were at the baker's right on the dot of 7:30. The short paddle back to camp with the aroma of the freshly baked buns in their nostrils had their mouths watering even before they were able to fry up a couple of eggs and some bacon to go with them. They both agreed that the fresh buns were even better than the ones they had the night before, and neither had any trouble eating their two apiece.

After cleanup, they watched the channel for about an hour until there appeared to be enough water flowing into the lagoon to allow the kayak to get through, and they set off.

This ride was really wild since the current was running at full force and they were in the light kayak on top of the waves. The boat bounced off a few rocks during the passage but sustained no damage. The boys and kayak were launched into the lagoon and were halfway to the island before they had to do any paddling.

"That was a hoot!" exclaimed Will. "I can't wait for the ride back out."

Chapter Twelve

33

"Once in the lagoon, they could see the little island..."

"I'm afraid you'll have to for a few hours," responded Michael. "But there should be plenty to see before it's time to head back."

There was indeed a lot to see in the lagoon. They spotted deer, raccoons, beavers, otters, and literally hundreds of birds. They beached the kayak on the little island in the middle and climbed to the top. The view was great, and except for the calls of the birds, it was totally still.

Time went by very quickly, and soon the current in the channel changed, and the boys knew they needed to run the rapids in the other direction. Going through the other way was just as much fun, and they decided to do the same round trip the next morning before their parents came to pick them up in the afternoon.

Returning to camp, they broke out lunch and sat on the beach to enjoy it. The rest of the day was spent taking the kayak into every nook and inlet in the cove.

By the time they had finished the spaghetti, garlic bread, sliced tomatoes, and the dozen cookies Angie had packed, along with another quart of milk, both were ready to sack out, even though it was still fairly light. They fell asleep to the sounds of laughter from the people on nearby boats and did not even pretend to watch the moon rise.

The next morning was a repeat of the previous one with the paddle to collect the cinnamon buns, making breakfast, and riding the rapids into the lagoon. By the time they returned to their camp and had some lunch, they started packing up their gear. They had pretty much broken camp when the Whaler appeared next to their little islet.

Both boys and parents had tales to tell of their adventures of the past two days, and the ride back to Quadra was a cheerful one. When they pulled up to the home float, Angie and Judy announced that as soon as the boys had unpacked and stowed all their gear they could come up for dinner.

Chapter Thirteen

Two days after the families returned from Cortes, Bob received a call from their friends with the large cruiser saying they would arrive on Quadra within the next forty-eight hours. They agreed to stay a couple of days before taking the boys and heading off north.

Michael moved the Whaler around to the end of the float to make room for the new arrivals while Will cleaned up the kayak so they could take it with them. Both boys packed duffle bags with clothes and other items they wanted to have on the northern journey, including their iPhones for picture-taking.

The big boat arrived right on schedule and brought with it a freshly caught salmon for that night's dinner. The boys had picked blackberries along the road and dug some clams for chowder, so a grand feast was put together in short order.

The couple on the cruiser, Harold and Jane, took to the boys immediately, and the feeling was mutual. They had mapped out quite a long cruise and went over the charts in detail with Michael and Will. It would be about two weeks long and cover a good portion of the region from Quadra up to the Broughton Archipelago. The plan was to head up through the islands due north from Quadra on the way to Mamalilaculla on Village Island. From there, they would circle back toward the mainland and Echo Bay and the Burdwood Group. Then they would swing out through Fife Sound, past Broughton Island,

Sutlej Channel
Sullivan Bay
Wells Passage
Broughton Island
Fife Sound
Cramer
Retreat P.
Queen Charlotte Strait
Mamali
Blackfish Sd.
Telegraph C.
Johnstone Strait

Chapter Thirteen

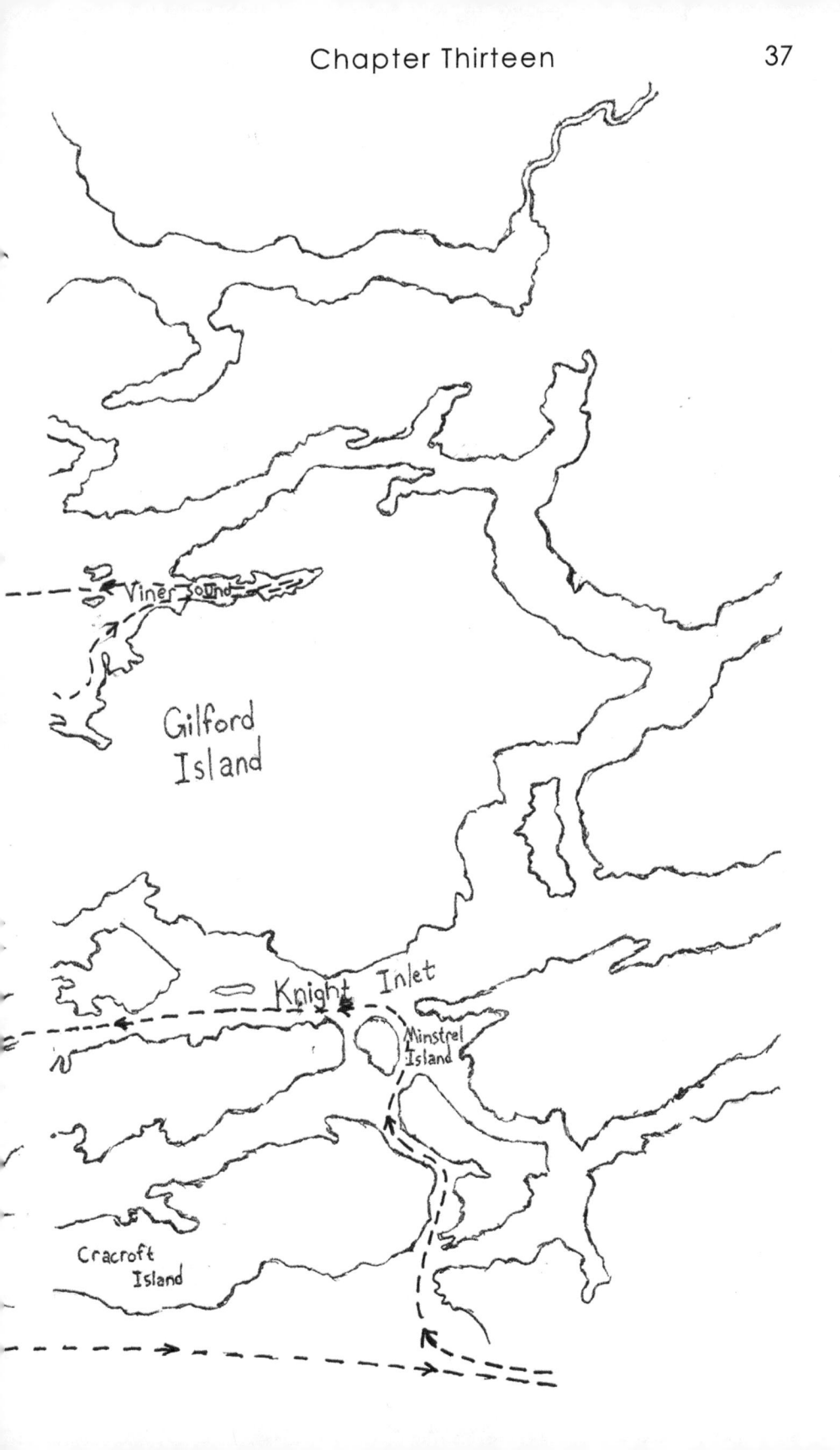

into the Queen Charlotte Strait, and back down to Blackfish Sound, Telegraph Cove, and down the Johnstone Strait back to Quadra.

Both Michael and Will were thrilled with the prospect of such a long adventure to places they could not possibly get to in the Whaler. Harold and Jane were happy to haul the two-man kayak along so the boys could do some exploring on their own at various moorages, and this made the trip even more special.

It was decided they would all share one more dinner together since Doug and Judy would have to return to Chicago before the boys returned. After breakfast the next morning, a major market trip was made to Heriot Bay. Angie and Judy warned Harold and Jane about the boys' appetites but explained they would be sent off with adequate provisions.

"Oh, don't worry about that," said Jane. "Our grandsons can probably match them bite for bite. Anyway, we'll gather some oysters and dig some clams before we go. We usually have good luck fishing, and we have both crab and prawn traps, so we can easily supplement the food supply."

"Besides, there are stores along the way," put in Harold. "Echo Bay, Sullivan Bay, and Telegraph Cove all have good provisions. Also, if the pie last night and the one I understand is on the menu for tonight are any evidence, I would bet these two could rustle up some fresh fruit along the way. If we're lucky, some cherry trees at Mamalilaculla may help us out, although we may have to fight the bears for them."

The trip to Heriot Bay resulted in steaks, baked potatoes, and a big Caesar salad for the main course. The blackberry pie was a huge hit, and everyone was groaning by the end of the meal.

An early departure the next morning was not necessary since they were going through Whiterock Passage on the way north and did not need to wait for the slack at Surge Narrows. This gave the boys one more chance at Angie's special pancakes, and Will had time to say good-bye to his parents.

The entire crew came down to the float for the sendoff. Jane showed the boys where to stow their gear and settle into their cabin. Matt used the davit to haul the two-man kayak up to the fly bridge and tied it down next to the dinghy. Just ahead of noon, they cast off the lines and headed out into Hyacinthe Bay on the grand adventure.

Chapter Fourteen

Whiterock Passage was as beautiful as the boys had remembered it, but it was certainly more of a navigational challenge in the large cruiser than it had been in the Whaler. Harold showed the boys how to line up the markers to make the turn about halfway through, and they emerged into Calm Channel.

They turned north up the channel along Sonora Island. Harold showed them on the chart the Yuculta Rapids between Sonora and Stuart Islands. They all could see ahead a wall of water in the middle of the channel much higher than what the boys had observed in Surge Narrows. Harold noted there were massive whirlpools just beyond the wall and even his boat was no match for them.

He turned instead just before Stuart Island and headed up Bute Inlet. "We'll cruise up Bute a ways and find a nice cove for our anchorage tonight. Tomorrow morning early, we'll motor farther up and see if we can spot some grizzly bears."

"Boy, that would be something!" said Will. "I've only seen them in the zoo. How close do you think we can get?"

"Not close enough to get us in any trouble," said Harold with a laugh.

"Just see that you stick to that," said Jane emphatically.

After about an hour of leisurely cruising, they spotted a perfect little place to anchor for the night. After setting the anchor, they lowered the dinghy, and Harold enlisted the boys to help with the stern tie. He then checked the depth sounder and announced that setting the prawn traps was in order. The boys helped put out the traps under Harold's watchful eye.

"This is the easy part," he informed them. "Hauling them up takes a lot more effort. We'll do that right before dinner, but I'll bet you two could use a little snack right about now."

"You won't get any argument from us," said Michael.

They returned to the cruiser and tied the dinghy up to the swim platform. Jane saw them coming and announced that lunch would be served in the main salon as soon as hands were washed.

After lunch, they took a little dinghy cruise along the shore of the inlet. They passed a few other boats, but it was quite peaceful. Grizzlies were not to be seen, but the four did see a number of other creatures and lots of eagles.

"That's a good sign," said Harold pointing to the eagles. "If they're here, there must be salmon running, and that means the bears are probably fishing."

Finally Jane said she needed to return to the boat to do some dinner preparation, so they turned around and headed back. They dropped Jane off at the boat and went out to check the prawn traps.

The boys learned exactly what Harold had meant about pulling them in. Three hundred feet of line took quite a while to haul in, trying to keep it from tangling in the process. They were amply rewarded, however, when the traps broke the surface. Each one had more than a dozen nice-size prawns.

"That will make a tasty lunch tomorrow or an appetizer before dinner," announced Harold. "Good work, lads!"

The prawns were secured to the swim platform in a bucket of seawater, and the boys went forward to lie on the deck in the warm sun. They were still relaxing when the dinner bell rang.

"Even with hauling in the prawn traps, I could really get used to this life," said Will.

"Me, too," said Michael, getting to his feet and heading into the main cabin.

The boys helped Jane clean up after dinner, and the four of them settled in to watch a movie before bed.

Chapter Fifteen

The four got an early start the next morning. Harold taught the boys how to raise the anchor and then showed them the special knot he used to easily release the stern tie without having to go to shore. Since they weren't moving particularly fast, they simply towed the dinghy. While the boys and Harold were getting them underway, Jane prepared a delicious breakfast, which they all enjoyed on the fly bridge watching the scenery pass by.

Harold told the boys he knew of a rather large stream that emptied into Bute Inlet and was home to a salmon run.

"If the eagles are any sign, there should be salmon in the stream and some grizzlies on the banks snagging their fill."

In less than an hour, they reached the place Harold had mentioned, and sure enough, while dozens of eagles circled overhead ready to swoop, two huge grizzly bears had waded into the stream and were scooping salmon out right and left. Both boys were mesmerized by the sight, and Harold maneuvered them in as close as he dared for a great view and dozens of photos.

"Those guys look even bigger than the ones in the zoo in Chicago," Will noted.

"The average male weighs in at about seven hundred pounds, but some have reached fifteen hundred," said Harold.

"I sure wouldn't want to run into one in the wild," said Michael.

"I wouldn't relish that prospect, either," said Harold. "However, if you do, I've been told that you either roll up in a ball and pretend to be dead or try to run uphill."

"Why uphill?" asked Michael. "I'd think you'd make better time running downhill."

"Perhaps that's true," said Harold. "However one of those guys would be much faster since they just run over anything in their path. You wouldn't stand a chance."

"Well, let's not have anyone here try to prove out that theory," said Jane.

During the excitement of watching the grizzlies and eagles vie for salmon, Will happened to glance up into the trees along the shore.

"Wow, would you take a look at that eagle in the big fir? He has got to be the great granddaddy of all time."

"I think you must be right," said Harold. "I don't ever recall seeing one that big."

"Why doesn't he join in with the rest of them going after the salmon?" asked Michael. "He looks as if he could grab just about anything he wanted, short of one of the bears, of course."

"I surely don't know" said Harold.

They continued watching the bears for an hour or so, Harold mentioned that Yuculta should be calm in another hour or so and they should make their way back and cruise by Dent Island and look for another moorage for the night.

They hit the tide right at Dent and proceeded around the north side of East Thurlow Island, where they found a beautiful and completely deserted cove for their moorage. It was so nice that they decided to spend two nights there and lowered the kayak so the boys could go off and do a little exploring.

Harold and Jane went off in the dinghy and found some shallows with lots of eel grass, a favorite habitat of Dungeness crabs, so they returned to the boat and dug out the pots. By the time the boys returned from the paddling adventure, there was a bucket of six large crabs on the swim platform.

The boys sat on the platform with Harold and broke the heads off the shrimp landed the day before while Jane put water on to boil for cooking the shellfish. Dinner that night consisted of a mound

Chapter Fifteen

43

"...two huge grizzly bears had waded into the stream..."

of shrimp and crab, a big green salad, and a loaf of French bread. Nobody even missed dessert.

The next day was spent exploring more of the area around the cove and planning where the next stop would be. The boys were really getting into gunkholing, or searching out small isolated moorages.

They mapped out a course to get them to Minstrel Island in two leisurely days of travel. From there, they would cruise down Knight Inlet to Mamalilaculla on Village Island.

Jane had a nice collection of books on the area, including both *Heart of the Rainforest*, which the boys had read the year before, *The Raven Steals the Light*, which they had just read, and *The Curve of Time*, which was new to them, but Jane said she had read it at least three times. It told the story of a woman, her children, and a couple of dogs who sailed the entire region they were now exploring back in the mid-1950s.

Both Will and Michael found the book fascinating and took turns reading during the days' cruises. While they both observed that much had probably changed in the past sixty years, it was amazing how much remained the same and unspoiled.

"That's what we love so much about this area," Jane said. "There are certainly some encroachments of civilization, but you really feel you have gotten away from it all when you come here."

When they reached Minstrel Island, Harold cruised on past and found moorage off a small island across from a marina at Lagoon Cove. It was late afternoon when they took the dinghy into the marina and checked out the little store on the dock. The marina was only about half full, but the boaters who were there had pretty much cleaned the shelves. They were able to buy some candy bars and potato chips, but that was about it.

Fortunately, the evening before, Harold and Jane had done some fishing while the boys were relaxing and reading, and they had caught two perfect "eating size" salmon. Harold cleaned them and put one in the freezer for later, and the other provided the main course for this night.

The next morning, they motored down Knight Inlet toward Village Island. They found a secluded cove just across from Mamalilaculla

Chapter Fifteen 45

and set the anchor deciding to take the dinghy across the channel the next day to spend time exploring the historic site.

Chapter Sixteen

Over breakfast, Harold and Jane told the boys a little more about the site.

"When we first came here," Jane began, "a group of volunteers conducted tours of the area and explained what the potlatches were all about and how they had been outlawed by the government in the early 1920s. Now it seems they are just letting the village return to the soil."

"There were First Nations people inhabiting this site for probably thousands of years, based on the height of the midden, which is about twelve feet high," added Harold.

"There really isn't a lot left to see, but there may be something of an old fallen totem, which we saw two years ago. Most of the structures built here have fallen down, but there are a few left standing. On the other side of the island are more buildings, which at various times served as a school and hospital. There is also a dock, but it's long since passed as being serviceable, which is why we need to take the dinghy in," added Jane.

The boys were excited to experience a real-life history lesson and eagerly gathered up whatever gear they thought they might need for the visit, including, of course, their iPhones for photos. Based on the possibility of finding the cherry orchard mentioned by Harold, they also packed a couple of collapsible pails. Jane told them that should they prove successful she would whip up a cherry pie for dessert.

Chapter Sixteen

They motored across the calm channel to the broad midden in front of what had been the village. The bottom was rather muddy, but they pulled the dinghy up and secured it with a line far up on the beach.

Wandering around the village, they saw the remains of the totem they had talked about at breakfast. It was really overgrown with vines, but the carving was still in evidence, and the boys snapped a few photos. They also detected the remains of an old longhouse and the gateway used in the last potlatch.

"These should be interesting pictures for my class next year," noted Will.

"I'll bet there's one member who will get a private showing," said Michael with a smile, giving Will a playful poke in the arm.

"Why don't we take a hike to the other side of the island," suggested Will, trying to change the subject.

"The trail is back this way," said Harold, pointing. "The cherry orchard is off to one side. If they're ripe, we can stop to pick on the way back."

As the four wandered through the brushy trail, they could see some bright red fruit on the trees, so the picking side trip was promptly scheduled for the return. The old buildings that had served as former institutions of a later age were also in a state of obvious neglect, but the crew did take peeks inside. There weren't any photo-ops for the boys, so they shortly turned back and made for the orchard.

Jane said she did not want to wade into the weeds and climb some trees so told Harold and the boys she would wait for them on the beach.

Pushing through the bushes, the three of them reached the orchard. Harold picked from the ground, but the boys decided to climb up a couple of the larger trees where they could see bigger cherries. With all of them picking, they were able to secure enough fruit for a good-size pie. The boys came down from the trees, and they all were just about ready to head back to meet Jane when they heard a rather large rustling in the bushes coming toward the orchard.

Harold told the boys that they were about to have a genuine wildlife encounter and to make some significant noise. Michael and Will looked a little puzzled but did as they were told. The rustling ceased for a moment but then started up again. Harold motioned for the boys to head back toward the trail but to keep up the noise. They had just about reached the trail when they saw a large black mass moving through the brush.

"That, boys," said Harold, pointing, "is a real, live young black bear coming in for some fresh fruit of his own."

"Wow!" said the boys simultaneously.

Quickly handing their pails of cherries to Harold, they whipped out their iPhones and began snapping away.

"I think it would be a good idea for us to move on out and leave our friendly bruin to his snack before he decides to be unfriendly," said Harold emphatically.

The boys wanted to keep taking pictures, but Harold finally put a hand on each shoulder and gently moved them back onto the trail. They could hardly contain themselves in relating the story to Jane, who noted that she was happy to have missed the experience but did say they had certainly earned a pie for dessert.

Chapter Seventeen

Dinner that evening was an animated affair with the bear encounter dominating conversation. The pie was the star of the meal and was almost completely consumed. By the time the sun set, they were all ready for bed, deciding to sketch out the future cruising plan over breakfast the next morning.

After a really good night's sleep and a hearty breakfast, the charts were spread out on the table. Harold noted that it would take them at least three days of easy cruising to make it to Echo Bay and the Burdwoods, so they opted to pass around Gilford Island through Retreat and Cramer Passes.

The dinghy and kayak were hauled up to the fly bridge, the stern tie released, and the boys pulled up the anchor. They cruised through waters dotted with what seemed to be hundreds of tiny islets and found wonderful, secluded coves for moorages. Harold and Jane caught a few more salmon and even hauled in a small halibut, so fantastic fresh seafood dinners were the norm for this part of the trip.

By the time they reached Echo Bay, there were some other supplies needed, so they pulled into the marina and made their way to the store, which was far better stocked than the one at Lagoon Cove. Jane took care of the shopping list and told the men to make a trip across the bay to the bakery, a suggestion readily agreed to by all three of them, so they returned to the cruiser and lowered the dinghy.

Harold noted that the next moorage he wanted to make was not far off, so they could simply tow the dinghy.

With multiple bags of groceries and baked goods to store, they decided to spend one night tied up in the marina and head out in the morning. Harold pointed out to the boys that the large float that housed the market was actually on one of the pontoons of the old floating bridge across Lake Washington in Seattle.

The boys then had the chance to point out to their hosts the house that belonged to Billy Proctor, the subject of *Heart of the Rainforest*, so they were all able to share interesting facts.

The next morning, they headed off for the short cruise to Viner Sound, where Harold wanted to spend the night. They slowly motored all the way to the end of the sound, where a stream emptied into it. There were no other boats around, so Harold decided not to do a stern tie but just swing at anchor.

As they sat relaxing on the fly bridge in the late afternoon, the boys suddenly spotted several dorsal fins moving in the sound.

"Look," said Michael, "dolphins!"

They watched the dolphins swim around for quite a while, and then it was Will's turn to make an announcement.

"Check out the little creek," he said excitedly.

They all turned to see a mother black bear with two cubs wading in the shallow water.

"Now this is my idea of a bear sighting," said Jane.

The boys were able to get some more great wildlife photos and wanted to make a quick call back to their parents, but they had absolutely no cell phone coverage.

"You'll probably have to wait till we get to Telegraph Cove on the way home to make your calls," observed Harold. "Tomorrow, we'll go out to the Burdwood Group. I want to show you a beautiful white shell midden that, when looked at through the water, makes you think you're in the Caribbean."

"Why don't we go into Simoom Sound and find a moorage there and then take the dinghy back to the Burdwoods?" suggested Jane.

"That's a great idea," agreed Harold. "We can also lower the kayak when we get anchored so the boys can explore the sound when we return from the Burdwoods."

Chapter Seventeen

"...a mother black bear with two cubs..."

"That sounds great," said Michael. "I want you to know this has been an absolutely fantastic trip so far. I'm so happy we were able to join you."

"I second that thought completely," said Will. "Thank you both!"

"You boys are very welcome," said Harold. "I've appreciated the help you've been in mooring and other chores on the boat."

"I'm sure you'll have a few more sights and adventures to report before we get back to Quadra," said Jane.

Chapter Eighteen

Harold pointed out the Burdwood Group as they passed by on their way to Simoom Sound. The sound was quite large, and there were a number of boats already at anchor when they arrived. They found a quiet area, set the anchor, secured the stern tie, lowered the kayak, grabbed a bite of lunch, and headed off in the dinghy for the Burdwoods.

The white shell midden was exactly as advertised. The shells extended quite a ways from the shore and, when viewed through the water, gave it a turquoise tinge, making it look just like a beach in the Bahamas.

They explored the island and then returned to the boat. Harold and Jane went into the sound and set the crab pots in a small cove and the prawn traps out in the deep part of the sound.

The boys hopped aboard the kayak, taking along their collapsible buckets, and said they would try to find some huckleberries. Paddling into the far end of the sound, they found a small beach, so they pulled the kayak up on shore and walked into the low shrubbery. Not far in, they found a trove of huckleberry bushes and filled the two buckets in less than an hour. As they loaded their booty into the kayak and cast off from shore Will looked back at the little beach and the woods rising behind it. In another large fir, right at the top he spied a huge eagle.

"That has got to be the same eagle we saw in Bute Inlet."

"I think you're right," said Michael. "I wonder why he's here, there sure aren't any salmon around. Eagles are supposed to be rather territorial, and this is quite a ways away from where we first saw him."

Returning to the cruiser, they presented Jane with their booty, and she promised a pie for the evening, noting that there would be plenty of berries for pancakes in the morning. They mentioned to Harold about seeing what they thought must be the same giant eagle they had seen at Bute Inlet, and Harold echoed the sentiment that it seemed to be a bit out of what would normally be his territory, assuming it was the same eagle.

As evening approached, Harold and the boys went out to retrieve the crab pots and prawn traps and were richly rewarded on both counts. Both Will and Michael agreed the sore arms from hauling in the catch were well worth the absolutely fresh seafood.

The next day's cruise was up the eastern shore of Broughton Island, past Greenway Sound, through the Sutlej Channel, and past Sullivan Bay. They stopped in at the marina in Sullivan Bay for lunch in the little café on the dock and then proceeded into Wells Passage, where they found a wonderful moorage for the night.

During the evening's shellfish feed, Harold announced that they had come about as far north as they were planning to go and they would start the cruise back to Quadra. Noticing the fallen faces of the two teenagers, Jane offered them some solace.

"It'll take us at least four or five days to get back, so the adventure isn't over yet."

"We'll spend another night here around Broughton Island before heading across the Queen Charlotte Strait to the northern shore of Vancouver Island and into Telegraph Cove," said Harold. "We have to watch the weather pretty carefully for the crossing because it is really open water and can get rougher than I like to sail in."

Harold pulled out the charts and showed the boys their return route. He pointed out a large bay on Broughton Island where he planned to spend the next night and noted there were dozens of small islets the boys could explore in the kayak.

"Unless we have just the right weather, we can stay here an extra night," he said, and the boys brightened a bit, hoping for a bit of a squall to come up.

Chapter Eighteen

They got an early start the next morning and reached the moorage spot before lunchtime. With the cruiser swinging at anchor in the large bay, both the dinghy and kayak were lowered and tied on the stern. Jane prepared a delicious lunch, after which the boys were anxious to go off exploring. Harold and Jane said they would break out the fishing tackle and try to land some fresh fish for dinner.

Chapter Nineteen

Both groups headed back out toward the mouth of the bay. Harold and Jane continued out into Fife Sound to do their fishing, but the boys surveyed the many small islands around the mouth of the bay.

"Have you ever seen so many beautiful places with absolutely no people?" asked Michael as they slowly paddled among the islands.

"Certainly not in Chicago," replied Will.

"It would be fun to get a better overview of this area," said Michael. "Let's scout out the highest of these small islands and see if we can find someplace to beach the kayak and then hike up to the top."

"That sounds like fun. What about that one over there?" said Will, pointing to a tiny island that stuck up almost like an obelisk from the water.

"I would say that's a perfect choice. Let's see if we can find a little beach."

On the far side of the island, they found a strip of sand with a gradual slope up from it. They brought the kayak ashore and hauled it up past the high-tide line and tied it to a tree.

The gradual slope soon turned into a much steeper climb, but there was not a lot of underbrush, so the way up was easier than it might have been. Still, the trek took quite some time since there was no actual trail to follow.

"I wonder how many people have climbed up this rock," said Will.

"I'd bet not very many. There was certainly no sign anyone had camped here that we could see as we went around it, and that beach was no midden, so there wouldn't have ever been a settlement here."

As they looked up the slope, they could see what looked to be somewhat of a clearing at the top, and they made their way toward it. They came out through some bushes into what almost looked like a park.

"Oh my gosh!" exclaimed Will. "Do you see what I see?"

"I'm sure I do, but I'm not exactly sure what it is you're looking at," replied Michael.

"That tree in the middle of the clearing! It's a golden spruce!"

"OK, I see it's a pretty unusual color, but what of it?"

"There was an old Haida legend of the golden spruce. I read about it on the Haida Nation website but didn't include it in my paper because I already had more than enough material."

"So what did the legend say?"

"As well as I can remember, the tree was unique and was created when a young boy ignored his grandfather's advice and turned around to look at his old village, which was destroyed. When he turned around, his feet took root and he became the golden spruce as a lesson to the Haida people to respect the land and sea and all creatures."

"But we're way south of where the Haida were based, so this couldn't be that tree."

"No, it definitely couldn't be that tree since someone cut that one down as a protest of big timber logging practices back in 1997, but there have never been any others found."

"That's really weird. How do you think this one got here?" asked Michael.

"I have absolutely no idea, but let's get some pictures to take back with us. Maybe when we get to someplace with satellite Internet coverage, we can look up the legend and get more information. I definitely want to ask Robert Bringhurst about it when we get back to your place."

"It's so funny this tree is right in the middle of this clearing. It's almost as if someone planted it here on purpose. If it was supposed to be a message, you'd think they'd plant it somewhere more obvious."

"That tree in the middle of the clearing! It's a golden spruce!"

Chapter Nineteen

"Maybe they were worried that the same thing would happen to this one if it was found. Or then again, maybe it simply grew here on its own."

"Well, there's no question it is a real mystery," said Michael. "Let's get back to the boat and show the pictures to Harold and Jane. Maybe they know something about it."

As the boys were preparing to work their way back down the slope, they cast their eyes up into the upper branches of the golden spruce.

"Oh my gosh!" exclaimed Will. "That's the eagle up there! What is he doing here?"

"I don't have any idea," said Michael, "But it's almost as if he's been following us."

As the boys left the clearing heading back down to the beach, Eagle rose from the golden spruce. With questions swirling around in their heads, and Eagle circling over them, the boys launched the kayak and paddled back to the boat.

Chapter Twenty

The boys found Harold cleaning fish at a table he had set up on the swim platform.

"Hail to the explorers," he called out warmly. "We got skunked on the salmon but found an underwater rock pillar that was just crawling with rockfish, so we hauled in a few. If you've never had fresh-caught fish and chips, you are in for a real treat."

"We're game for anything you and Jane want to serve up," said Will. "But we've returned with a mystery we hope you might be able to solve."

"Just let me finish these last two fish, and I'll give your mystery my undivided attention. I really need to pay a mind to cleaning these rockfish. See these spines? They can put a big hole in your hand if you aren't careful."

When Harold had finished with the last of the fish, he threw the skin and innards overboard for the dogfish and laid out ten filets of beautiful white fish. The boys helped clean up and stow the table and carry the filets into the galley, where Jane was at work making a big batch of coleslaw.

"OK, lads, what's the big mystery?" asked Harold slipping into a comfortable chair in the salon.

"Have you heard of the Haida legend of the golden spruce?" Will began.

Chapter Twenty

"I recall something about a golden spruce tree, but I'm not familiar with any legend. What about you, Jane? Does it ring a bell with you?"

"There was a book that came out maybe five to ten years ago about that tree. I think some logger cut it down as a form of protest, but that's all I remember."

"Well, we found another golden spruce," Will went on. "We have pictures. Michael, let them have a look."

"That's amazing," exclaimed Harold.

"Never in my life have I seen an evergreen so obviously NOT green," added Jane.

"While I was doing a paper on the Haida for my social studies class, I went on the Haida Nation's website and found the story of the legend. The tree grew from the body of a young boy who disobeyed his grandfather, and it was revered by the Haida as a message to respect their surroundings. They actually named the tree, which was unique in Haida culture. I don't think I have all the details of the legend exactly right, but we can check it out when we get someplace with satellite Internet."

"The real mystery around the particular tree we found today is how it got there. Its position in a clearing right on top of an uninhabited island makes it look as if someone had planted it there on purpose," put in Michael.

"If it was planted as a reminder of the legend and the message about preserving the environment, though, why would someone put it in such a remote site?" added Will.

"The eagle we've been seeing was also there," said Michael. "what would explain that?"

"Those are all very good questions," observed Harold. "I wish we could help to shed some light on them, but you have us stumped as well."

"If we do have Internet in Telegraph Cove, I'll email Robert Bringhurst, a neighbor of Michael's, who is an expert on Haida culture."

"All this thinking has sure stirred up my appetite," said Michael. "Do you need a hand with those fish and chips?"

"I'll make up my special batter for the fish," said Harold. "I'll bet Jane could use some help peeling and slicing potatoes."

"If you boys take on that task, I'll see about whipping up a batch of chocolate cupcakes for dessert," Jane added.

With all hands pitching in on the dinner preparations, they were sitting down to eat within an hour. The boys agreed the meal was absolutely the best fish and chips they had ever eaten and kept going until the very last bite of fish was gone.

They all adjourned to the fly bridge to enjoy the gorgeous sunset and fresh-out-of-the-oven cupcakes. No one missed the fact they were not even frosted.

Chapter Twenty-One

The boys awoke the next morning with very mixed feelings. Both wanted the boating trip to go on as long as possible, but they now had a burning mystery before them, and the best prospects for solving it lay back on Quadra Island.

However, when they came into the salon for breakfast, they found the decision had already been made.

"I just checked the weather forecast for the next five days, and we basically have just today to get across the Queen Charlotte Strait," Harold announced. "Winds and seas are going to pick up by this evening, and I want to get us tucked in safely in Telegraph Cove."

The crew enjoyed a delicious waffle breakfast and then prepared to lift anchor and make a quick dash across the strait. The dinghy and kayak were hauled up and lashed down, just in case the weather arrived ahead of schedule, and they were under way before ten.

The crossing was smooth, although the waves began to pick up just as they reached Blackfish Sound, but the final leg into the cove was still pleasant. Harold had radioed ahead and secured a spot in the marina for the night and had also made reservations at a restaurant to give Jane a break from the galley.

They were tied up at the dock in plenty of time for their dinner reservation, so the boys checked to see if there was Internet coverage. It was slow but available. Michael went first and sent a brief email to his parents telling them what a great time they were having, and then he turned the computer over to Will.

Will had thought quite a bit about what he would say to Robert Bringhurst in his email and had even written it out before keying it in, so he would make sure to cover all the points of their discovery. He summed up by asking if Mr. Bringhurst would reach out to some of his contacts within the Haida community to see what their reaction might be. He attached the photos they had taken of the golden spruce and gave him the location of the island.

After sending the email, the boys washed up, changed clothes, and headed to the restaurant. Bob and Doug had foreseen the possibility of a dinner out during the trip and had provided their sons with money to treat their hosts. Harold and Jane were surprised but graciously accepted the boys' offer, and all enjoyed a festive meal ashore.

When they returned to the boat, Will checked his emails to see if there was one from Robert Bringhurst. He was delighted to find one and shared it with the others.

> Dear Will,
>
> It is good to hear from you and that you are up in our little part of the world.
>
> I found your photos fascinating. Although I have examined many of the Haida legends, I have to admit that the golden spruce was one I had little knowledge of until Grant Hadwin cut the tree down in 1997.
>
> I know there had been several attempts to clone the tree but was unaware that any had been successful. In any case, the size of the tree you have discovered indicates that it started growing perhaps several hundred years before the other was cut, which does make it rather mysterious.
>
> I have contacted several Haida elders and told them of your find and also gave them the location you

provided. It is my understanding that they will go to the island to view the tree themselves and then come here to Quadra.

They would very much like to meet you and your cousin and talk to you. Please let me know when you will return to Quadra, and I will set up a meeting.

Very truly yours,

Robert Bringhurst

    Both Will and Michael were thrilled with the news, and Harold and Jane congratulated them on what was apparently an historic discovery. Harold told the boys they would probably be back home in about three days and asked if they would like to spend one night in the Octopus Group on the way.
    Both Will and Michael were delighted with the prospect of revisiting the islands and readily agreed.
    "Can we put up a mobile in the little shack?" asked Michael, referring to the deserted building they boys had discovered in the Octopus Group that was festooned with mobiles created by boaters over the years.
    "Of course," replied Jane. "We did put one up about five years ago, but I think a new one is in order."
    "You two can put together a collection of items you want to include," said Harold. "We'll be there the day before we get back and have plenty of time to assemble the mobile before we get there."

Chapter Twenty-Two

The next day dawned bright and clear, the forecasted rough weather getting stalled off the Queen Charlotte Islands. The foursome cast off from the marina and headed out into the Johnstone Strait. Motoring past Cracroft Island, they noticed ahead what appeared to be a large flotilla of boats of all descriptions.

Harold flipped the radio over to Channel 16 and picked up a lot of chatter among boats. He turned up the volume and called the others up to the fly bridge.

"It looks as if there is quite a group of orcas up there. From what I can pick up off the radio, it appears there may be four or five pods. We'll cut our speed and sort of merge into the group."

They approached slowly and could see many dorsal fins and spouts. There were so many, they couldn't possibly count them. Over the radio came an announcement from a large whale watching charter boat among the group that they were going to drop a hydrophone over the side and broadcast the whale song on Channel 17.

Harold immediately switched the radio, and they were greeted with the amazing sounds of probably fifty killer whales communicating. The boys were spellbound.

"That has got to be about the most fantastic thing I've ever seen—and heard!" exclaimed Will. "We sure don't get this in Chicago."

"We don't get something like this around here very often, either," noted Harold.

Chapter Twenty-Two

They drifted with the flotilla for almost an hour as the orcas made their way down the strait. They passed West Thurlow Island, and Harold turned into the channel between it and East Thurlow. He said he had a nice anchorage in mind for that night, and they would proceed to the Octopus Group the next day and then on home the day after.

Harold found the cove he wanted and noted it had really good crabbing, so they dropped the anchor, lowered the dinghy, and set the pots. Within two hours, they were rewarded with eight big Dungeness crabs and prepared for a feast that night.

After dinner, the boys set about putting together the mobile they planned to hang the next night in the little shack in the Octopus Group. Harold told them it would be an easy cruise the next day, so they could sleep in, which everyone did.

The next morning, they went back out into the Johnstone Strait and proceeded around the western shore of Sonora Island and then into the Okisollo Channel and on to the Octopus Group. They found a perfect place to anchor, secured the stern tie, and lowered the dinghy. After a relaxed lunch, they all boarded the dinghy and headed off to the shack for the official hanging of the mobile.

Everything seemed the same as when the boys had visited the year before, and Jane pointed out the mobile she and Harold had hung up five years earlier. They all agreed that this new creation was a masterpiece and would surely be admired by all who came here for many years to come.

With this major artistic contribution in place, they explored the channels around the many small islands of the group before returning to the boat. Remembering they had cell phone coverage here, Michael called his parents to let them know they would be arriving the next day.

Harold had checked the tides at Surge Narrows and said they would be back at the float on Quadra by about two in the afternoon. Bob and Angie asked that they give them a call when they rounded the Bretons, so they could meet the boat when it docked.

The boys expressed regret that the cruise was coming to an end, but they were also extremely excited about the pending meeting with Robert Bringhurst and the Haida elders.

To celebrate their last night on the boat, Jane put together another batch of chocolate cupcakes and, this time, even whipped up a bowl of very rich frosting.

Chapter Twenty-Three

As they came through Surge Narrows, the boys pointed out the cove where they had discovered the stolen logs last summer. After emerging from the narrows, they also described in detail the experience with the log pirates who tried to ram and sink them. Harold and Jane were amazed at the story, and it became the topic of discussion for the rest of the cruise down to the float on Quadra.

Michael did place the call to his parents as they rounded the Bretons. Bob and Angie were on the float when the boat pulled up, and they helped secure the lines. Harold lowered the kayak, and the boys climbed aboard, paddled it up to the boathouse, and put it away.

Angie told them Bob had dug a big batch of clams and a kettle of chowder was on the stove. She added that some freshly baked sourdough rolls had just come out of the oven, along with a several dozen chocolate-chip cookies.

The boys gathered up their gear from the boat, dropped it off in the caboose, and were in the kitchen, appetites intact, almost before their parents and Harold and Jane had arrived.

Over bowls of delicious chowder, soaked up with more than a few fresh rolls, tales of the nautical journey were related, including bear and orca encounters and, of course, the discovery of the golden spruce. Will showed the group the photos he had taken with his iPhone. While they were going over the past several weeks, Michael brought out to the table his laptop and went on the Haida Nation's website so all could see the clever puppet show depicting the original legend of the golden spruce.

When the boys finally ran out of steam telling their stories, Will excused himself and looked up the number for Robert Bringhurst in the little Quadra telephone directory. He placed the call and had a brief conversation with the author. When he returned to the others, he announced that Mr. Bringhurst had a group of four Haida elders on the island and they would like to meet the next day around noon.

"Uncle Bob and Aunt Angie, I hope you don't mind, but I invited them to come here."

"That's absolutely no problem," Angie said. "I would like to meet our famous neighbor."

"Can you stick around for another day, or do you need to head south?" Bob asked Harold and Jane.

"If we are welcome to stay on your float, we would very much like to listen in on the meeting," Harold answered for them both.

"Then it's settled," said Bob. "Will, do you need to get back to Mr. Bringhurst to confirm?"

"I said I would after I checked with you, so I'll go do that now."

When he returned from the phone call, Will had another request.

"Mr. Bringhurst told me that the elders had asked that we not meet inside the house but on the beach, and I told him I was sure that would be OK with you."

"That'll be just fine," said Bob. "The tide should be still going out about noon, so you'll have plenty of time before it comes back in."

"Why don't we plan on a late breakfast," suggested Angie. "I don't know what this group might want for lunch, but I can ask when they get here, and we can make arrangements accordingly."

With a great deal of anticipation, the boys busied themselves for the rest of the day getting resettled into the caboose and collecting their clothes to be washed. They went down to the beach in front of the house and made sure there would be enough places for people to sit and rearranged a few beach logs.

Will finally made some time to call his parents, who had returned to Chicago shortly after the boys had left on their northern cruise. They were delighted to hear from him with his tales of adventures. Judy was a little concerned about the encounter with the black bear

Chapter Twenty-Three

on Mamalilaculla, but Will reassured her they had not been in any great danger.

When he finally got off the phone, it was nearly time for dinner, after which the whole crew made it an early night looking forward to the next day.

Chapter Twenty-Four

Promptly at noon the following day, a car pulled into the drive, and out stepped a tall, distinguished man accompanied by four truly elder members of the Haida Nation in traditional garb. The four elders each carried rolled up mats and several carved boxes.

Introductions were made all around, and the guests were shown to the stairs and trail down to the beach below the house. Very little conversation took place during the walk to the beach. When they all arrived, one of the elders scraped a shallow depression in the fine gravel beach while another gathered some dry driftwood. A small fire was laid in the depression, and mats were spread on the beach.

Bob, Angie, Harold, and Jane all took up spots on the logs the boys had arranged the previous day, and the rest sat on the mats around the fire pit. The wood smoke added a special ambiance to the gathering.

When they were all settled, one of the elders addressed the boys.

"We have traveled here from Haida Gwaii because of your remarkable discovery. We stopped by the site on our way to confirm what your photographs showed. Since the two of you are probably the first humans to observe the golden spruce, we want to ask you what you think is the significance of what you have found."

"Will has done far more research on this than I have," said Michael. "He should probably answer that question. I'll add anything that comes to mind after he has spoken."

Chapter Twenty-Four

"My research into your legends and culture is very rudimentary," Will began. "My knowledge of the legend of the golden spruce is totally drawn from your website and some excerpts from a book by John Valliant about the cutting down of the tree."

The elders simply nodded, so Will went on, "It is obvious from the size of the tree we found that it had been growing for many years before the other one was cut down. Also, since it is not in Haida Gwaii, it could not have any direct connection to the original legend."

Again the elders nodded and motioned for Will to continue.

"It is certainly a mystery as to the location of this tree, both on this small uninhabited island and in the clearing at the top, where it appears to have been planted, although, if it were planted, that simply compounds the mystery—planted by whom and for what purpose? I have thought about this quite a bit since we found the tree and have come to a conclusion. I hesitate to offer this conclusion since I have so little to base it on."

At his point, Robert Bringhurst spoke, "Will, I want to assure you that these gentlemen and I have been discussing this ever since you emailed me the photos and the location. Please know that we are as mystified as you by the questions you just posed. However, since you have the advantage of coming upon this tree first, your impressions are as valid as anyone else's."

"OK, just promise you won't laugh."

"That would be the farthest thing from our minds."

"Well, after viewing the story of the original legend several times, I don't think this tree has any connection to the mythical source of the first one, K'iid K'iyaas. I do believe, however, that it is directly connected to the lesson that was being imparted by the original legend."

At this, all the elders smiled and nodded, and one of them spoke, "You are wise beyond your years. We have come to the same conclusion. Who planted the tree is unimportant; it is the purpose that is important."

"There can be little question that the existence of the second golden spruce is intended as a reminder of the legendary lesson," said another of the elders.

"There is also no question in my mind," offered a third, "that the hand of Great Spirit was involved."

Finally Michael spoke up, "What is a question for me is why should we have been the ones to find the tree?"

The fourth elder turned to him and said, "You are the newcomers. You are the ones who need to spread the word of this lesson. Our people are becoming fewer every year, and many who remain do not subscribe to the old myths and legends. The old lessons are even more important today than they were hundreds of years ago."

"I guess I can see that," responded Michael. "We certainly have much more control over what happens to this area, for good or bad."

"You boys have just returned from a journey through some of the most beautiful country anywhere, but I am sure you saw some things to make you wonder what this all might look like in another hundred years," Robert Bringhurst added.

"We have somewhat of an idea," said Will. "Both of us have read *Heart of the Rainforest*, which details the many changes that have taken place in just the last seventy years."

"Things seem to be changing more quickly all the time," added Michael. "That's good in certain aspects of life, but it would be really sad to lose the natural beauty we've seen in these last two weeks."

"It is obvious to us that it will be up to your generation to make sure that does not happen," said one of the elders.

"It may sound like a small thing, Will, but your writing of a school paper on the subject of these ancient legends can be a good start," put in Robert Bringhurst. "It is especially important since it brings awareness in an area remote from where we are right now. I doubt many living in Chicago even know there is a people known as the Haida."

The discussion went on for a while longer with Harold, Jane, Bob, and Angie joining in as well with their thoughts. Finally, the conversation began to lag, and Angie spoke up. "I don't want to mention something so mundane in all this serious talk, but could I get something for lunch for everyone?"

"We have brought some offerings to share with you all," said one of the elders. He opened one of the beautifully carved boxes they had

Chapter Twenty-Four

carried down to the beach and took out some smoked salmon and various fruits and nuts and arranged it on the inside of the lid.

The group gathered around and partook of the traditional fare. The conversation lightened, but the elders continued to praise the boys for their insight and to thank them for sharing their discovery. They told them all that their intention was to make sure this golden spruce did not end up as a tourist attraction as had K'iid K'iyaas, and that its existence would be held within the Haida Nation.

One of the elders opened another box they had brought with them and pulled out two small parcels wrapped in plain paper. He handed one to each of the boys.

"These are tokens of our gratitude. We hope you will cherish them."

The boys unwrapped the gifts to find two intricately carved argillite totems. They were both awestruck and could barely say "thank you," but their appreciation was obvious, and the elders were pleased.

As the gathering on the beach was winding down, the fire doused, the mats rolled up, and the boxes resealed, Eagle gracefully rose from the tall fir from which he had been observing the meeting. He made one circuit of the little bay and then turned north.

Chapter Twenty-Five

After the guests had departed, Michael, Will, and the adults went out onto the deck and just sat enjoying the view across the water to Cortes Island and on to the Coast Range.

Finally, Bob said, "I don't want even to think about losing what we have here."

"It's not only here," observed Harold. "As the boys have now seen, there are miles of similar breathtaking wonder just a short distance away."

"The elders certainly laid a big challenge in your laps, boys," said Jane.

"I think we all need to take to heart what they said," said Angie. "We may not be the 'younger generation' anymore, but we can't simply put this all on our teenagers. After all, they weren't the ones who started making a mess of things."

"A point well taken," said Harold. "There are a lot of things we old folks can do."

"It's interesting they want to keep the golden spruce a secret," said Bob.

"I think I understand their motive," said Will. "After all, it's the lesson, or message, that's important here, not the tree itself. If they just turn it into another tourist attraction, they won't have accomplished much."

Chapter Twenty-Five

"You know," said Michael, "I think Will may have the makings here for another school report. As a matter of fact, I might give a shot at one myself."

"If you're lucky, you might even find a cute study mate to help out," said Will, with a laugh.

"Well, now that that's settled," said Angie, "maybe I should get started on some dinner."

"I think we'll be heading off south tomorrow," said Jane. "This morning I took a big slab of halibut we caught out of the freezer for a special going-away meal."

"That sounds perfect," said Angie. "Yesterday before you all arrived, one of our neighbors brought over some potatoes from her garden, along with just-picked lettuce and tomatoes. I'll do some scalloped potatoes and make a big salad. How do you want to cook the fish?"

"I have a special lime marinade I use," said Harold. "And then we can throw it on the barbeque wrapped in some foil."

"Will and I can go out on the road and pick some fresh blackberries for sundaes for dessert," said Michael.

"Well, I guess the rest of you have dinner taken care of, so I'll just sit here and continue to enjoy the view," said Bob. "Just let me know when you want me to fire up the grill."

Chapter Twenty-Six

The next day, the Quadra crew came down to the float to see off Harold and Jane and to wish them a safe journey home. As hugs and handshakes were being exchanged, Jane said, "This has been the most amazing trip. The boys were a great crew, and it was magic to see sights familiar to us through new eyes."

"Absolutely!" echoed Harold. "In all our years of cruising these waters, I can't think of a more enjoyable time, and what we learned from that group yesterday will stay with us the rest of our lives."

"Will and I also had a great time," said Michael. "You were marvelous hosts. We'd crew for you anytime. Thanks a bunch!"

"Michael's right," added Will. "I can't imagine having a better time, and that offer to crew goes double for me!"

After another round of hugs, the boys helped cast off the lines, and the cruiser pulled away from the float and headed out into Hyacinthe Bay. On the way back up to the house, both boys were very quiet.

"A bit of a letdown after all your excitement?" asked Bob.

"I guess so," said Michael. "We did have some pretty intense moments."

"Not as hair-raising as almost being tossed overboard as shark bait or being run down by a boat, but intense in a different way," noted Will.

"I think I can speak for your parents, Will, in saying this was a better kind of intensity," said Angie.

Chapter Twenty-Six

"I suppose so," said Will. "But this seems more important somehow."

"I get the same feeling," said Michael.

"It's just a sign of your growing maturity," observed Bob. "Two years ago, I don't think you would have been as receptive to what you learned on this trip."

The next few weeks were taken up with bike rides, hikes, kayak trips, and a couple of longer jaunts in the Whaler, including another overnighter to the Octopus Group, which had become a favorite place. The weather had started to change, and they even got nearly a week of rain, which put a damper on some of the outdoor activities. However, there were plenty of movies in Bob's collection, and they even got in a few much more competitive Monopoly games since Doug was in Chicago.

After the rain let up, they had sunshine again, but much lower temperatures. Angie announced to her two chowhounds that a neighbor had told her about a place to gather chanterelle mushrooms.

"They are really quite a delicacy. Would you like to go into the woods and see if we can find some?"

Always up for a new food treat, they readily agreed, and all four of them took off to the spot the neighbor had described. Bob parked the car off the road, and they got out the knives and small buckets they had thrown in the back.

"When we locate some," said Angie, "let me show you how to harvest them. You want to be careful to cut them off near the ground but not actually pull them up. That way, they will come right back after the next rain."

They had not gone far into the woods when Angie spotted a large group of the mushrooms and gave the boys their instructions. They then all wandered off in their separate directions in search of more. In less than an hour, among the four of them, they had quite a haul.

"OK, boys," said Angie, "when we get back, you get to clean them."

She sat the boys down on the deck with their knives and some small brushes and showed them how to clean the mushrooms. After a short time, she could hear moans coming from the deck and peeked out.

"You didn't tell us about this part," complained Michael. "This takes forever. Look, my fingers are all orange, and I haven't even gotten through one bucket."

"All right," said Bob, coming out onto the deck. "I'll lend a hand just to keep the noise level down out here."

At dinner, with a large helping of sautéed chanterelles piled on their steaks, the boys agreed that the cleaning had all been worth it.

Angie told them the mushrooms also made a great topping for scrambled eggs, so that became the plan for the next morning.

Chapter Twenty-Seven

In what seemed like no time at all, Bob had the boys helping to stow the deck furniture in the garage, getting the Whaler winterized, and cleaning and stowing the kayaks for the winter. Pulling out of the drive to go to the ferry was a sad moment for everyone, but the memories of a fantastic summer buoyed their spirits.

Will spent the night with Michael and his family before boarding the plane back to O'Hare. Before he left, however, he and Michael had already put together outlines of reports they were going to do for school in the coming year, now only about ten days away.

Will had even contacted his study mate in Chicago and sent her the outline to see if she would like to work on the project with him again. He had received an immediate positive response. He hadn't told her about finding the golden spruce but did direct her to the Haida Nation's website and told her to check out the legend and the book by John Valliant. She had emailed him back, "Why?" but he told her he would explain when he got back.

Will's parents met him at the airport and wanted to hear all about his meeting with Robert Bringhurst and the Haida elders. He related the entire story on the drive back downtown, and Doug and Judy were duly impressed.

Over the next week, he reconnected with his friends, played some baseball, and got into the mind-set for school, but he still had that eerie feeling that there were things he needed to do ...

Epilogue

In the time men refer to as the present, Eagle came before Great Spirit.

"I have done your bidding, Great Spirit. The new golden spruce has taken root and grown. I have watched over it for several lifetimes and have finally witnessed its discovery by two young newcomers."

"You have done well, my friend. What do you think are the intentions of these newcomers?"

"They appeared to hold the golden spruce in high regard. I followed them south from the archipelago, where they met with elders of your people."

"Yes, I observed my people visit the site where the tree now grows. They seemed pleased but mystified."

"That is very true, Great Spirit. They expressed as much in their meeting with the young newcomers. However, one of the newcomers seems to have grasped your message."

"This news is very reassuring. Were my people understanding?"

"They have pledged to keep the golden spruce away from the exploitation K'iid K'iyass experienced."

"This is indeed heartening. If both my people and the newcomers can learn from this, we will be in a better place."

"Will our forests and waters and wild creatures be safe?" asked Eagle.

Epilogue

"Only time can answer that, my friend, but if all men can show the wisdom of these few elders and these young newcomers, then we have hope."

Haida Eagle Symbol

Appendix

Will and Michael's Favorite Waffles

These are EVERYBODY'S favorite waffles.

Ingredients
4 eggs
2 cups sifted all-purpose flour
1 teaspoon salt
1 teaspoon baking soda
1 teaspoon baking powder
2 cups buttermilk (you may use dry buttermilk powder and water according to the instructions on the container)
1 cup butter, melted

Preheat waffle iron.

Beat eggs until light. Sift together flour, salt, baking soda, and baking powder. Add flour mixture and buttermilk alternately to the beaten eggs, beginning and ending with the flour mixture. Add melted butter and blend thoroughly. For each waffle, pour about ½ cup of batter into the center of the lower portion of the waffle iron until it spreads out to about 1 inch from the sides. The amount of batter to use will, of course, depend on the size of your iron. Cook according to the manufacturer's directions.

The author wishes to acknowledge ***The New Revised and Updated McCall's Cookbook*** (The McCall Publishing Company, 1984).

Squirrel Cove Cinnamon Buns

The marvelous bakery on the log raft in Squirrel Cove is a thing of the past, but the cinnamon buns will never be forgotten by anyone who ever had them.

Buns
> **Ingredients**
> 1½ packages dry yeast (about 3¼ teaspoons)
> ¼ cup warm water
> 1 cup milk
> ½ cup shortening
> ⅓ cup sugar
> 1½ teaspoons salt
> 1 egg, beaten
> 4–5 cups sifted all-purpose flour
> Melted butter
> Brown sugar*
> Cinnamon*
> 1 cup raisins, optional

* Quantities of these ingredients are left to the discretion of the chef, but don't be stingy! I make about a ½-inch thick layer of brown sugar and completely cover it with cinnamon.

Add the warm water to the yeast and soak for 10 minutes. Scald the milk; pour over shortening. Add sugar and salt and cool to tepid. Add dissolved yeast and egg. Add 4 cups of flour, one cup at a time, beating after each addition. Dough should be soft but firm enough to handle. Knead on a floured surface until elastic and smooth. Avoid adding too much flour. Turn dough into a well-oiled bowl and let rise for 1½ hours.

Press dough down and divide into workable size. Roll dough out into a rectangle and cover with melted butter. Layer with a generously thick layer of brown sugar, then sprinkle on cinnamon as desired (see note above), and add raisins if you like. Roll up jellyroll fashion. Using scissors or a piece of string or dental floss, cut off slices 1–1½ inches thick. Place slices in an 8- or 9-inch greased round cake pan, with one slice in the middle and the others around it. Press rolls down to even out and fill pan. Let rolls rise to generously fill pan, about 1 hour.

Bake in 350° oven for 15–20 minutes. If the rolls start to get too brown, cover with a piece of foil until the end of baking. Be careful not to overbake.

Remove immediately from pan by inverting onto a plate and then tipping over onto another plate to right the rolls. Spread with frosting (recipe follows).

Frosting
Ingredients
2 cups powdered sugar
1 tablespoon butter, melted
1 teaspoon vanilla extract
2–4 tablespoons milk or cream

In a medium bowl, place sugar, butter, and vanilla. Stir in enough milk or cream to reach a thick, hardly-able-to-stir consistency. Spread over warm rolls as soon as they are placed on a plate to let the frosting run into the rolls.

Other Bruce Bradburn Books

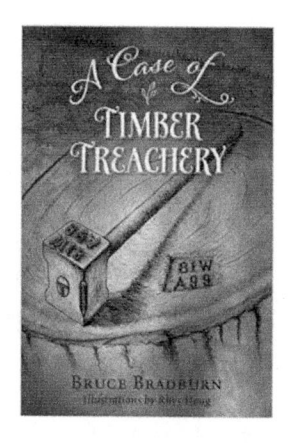

Both The Quadra Chronicles: an Otter Odyssey and A Case of Timber Treachery won The Best Children's Books of 2014. Out of all the children's books published in 2014, amazon.com editors pick the top 20 in each category for children of all ages.

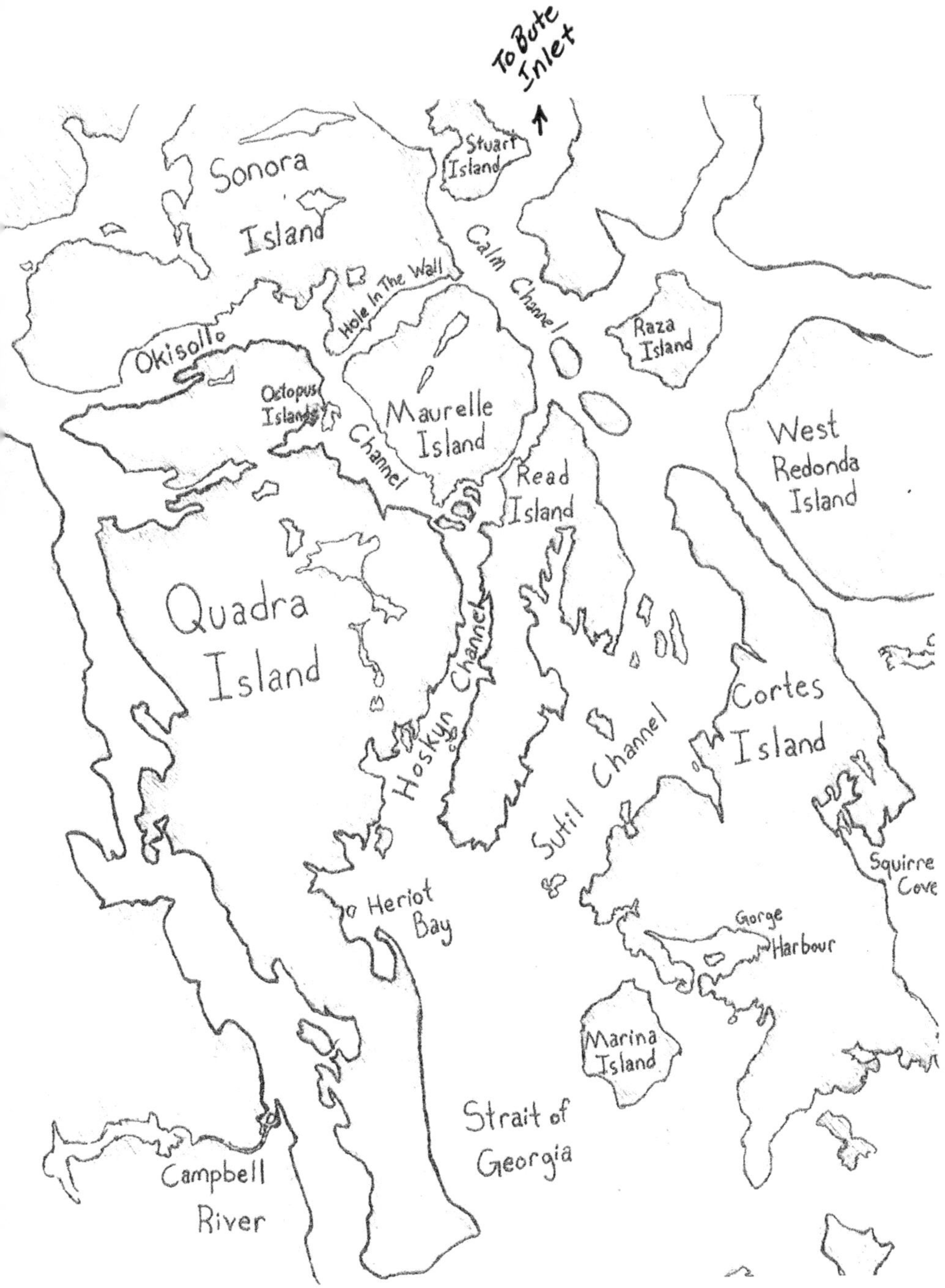
To Bute Inlet
Stuart Island
Sonora Island
Calm Channel
Hole In The Wall
Raza Island
Okisollo
Octopus Islands
Maurelle Island
Channel
West Redonda Island
Read Island
Quadra Island
Hoskyn Channel
Channel
Cortes Island
Sutil Channel
Squirre Cove
Heriot Bay
Gorge Harbour
Marina Island
Strait of Georgia
Campbell River